#37

Bijou

Also by Susan Hughes

Bailey

Riley

Murphy

Bijou

SUSAN HUGHES

sourcebooks
jabberwocky

Copyright © 2014 by Susan Hughes
Cover and internal design © 2017 by Sourcebooks, Inc.
Series design and illustrations by Jeanine Murch
Cover image © Medvedev Andrey/Shutterstock
Internal illustrations by Bill King

Published by Sourcebooks Jabberwocky, an imprint of Sourcebooks, Inc.
P.O. Box 4410, Naperville, Illinois 60567-4410
(630) 961-3900
Fax: (630) 961-2168
www.sourcebooks.com

Originally published as Bijou Needs a Home in 2014 in Canada by Scholastic Canada Ltd.

Library of Congress Cataloging-in-Publication Data
Names: Hughes, Susan, 1960- author.
Title: Bijou / Susan Huges.
Other titles: Bijou needs a home
Description: Naperville, Illinois : Sourcebooks Jabberwocky, [2017] | Series:
    Puppy pals ; 4 | "Originally published as Bijou Needs a Home in 2014 in
    Canada by Scholastic Canada Ltd." | Summary: When three bichon frise
    puppies are left at Tails Up, Kat worries that nobody will see the sweet,
    playful side of Bijou because he is shy.
Identifiers: LCCN 2015044667 | (alk. paper)
Subjects: | CYAC: Bichon frise--Fiction. | Dogs--Fiction. |
    Animals--Infancy--Fiction. | Bashfulness--Fiction.
Classification: LCC PZ7.H87396 Bi 2017 | DDC [E]--dc23 LC record available at
https://lccn.loc.gov/2015044667

Source of Production: Versa Press, East Peoria, Illinois, USA
Date of Production: December 2016
Run Number: 5008131

Printed and bound in the United States of America.
VP 10 9 8 7 6 5 4 3 2 1

For lovely, lively Leah Witten
and her rambunctious poodle Santo

K *at giggles. There are puppies everywhere! Some are tumbling in the grass. Some are chasing butterflies. Some are playing in the flower beds.*

Some puppies are white, some are brown, and some are red with spots. There are dachshunds and Afghans. There are Boston terriers and cocker spaniels.

There are too many puppies to count!

"Hey, Kat!" a voice said. "It's for you."

"Hey, Kat!" her brother Aidan says. "They're

for you, Sis. Any puppy you want. Mom and Dad have finally agreed." He punches her gently on the shoulder.

Kat grins. She can't believe it! It's a dream come true.

But which one should she pick? The sweet black-and-white border collie with the sparkling eyes? The Bernese mountain dog pup wagging its roly-poly body? The cute Labrador retriever with the white star on its black tummy?

"Hey, Kat!" It was her brother's voice again. "Sis!"

Kat was sitting at the computer in the living room. It was Saturday. Kat had been looking at photos of different breeds of puppies on the computer until she began daydreaming.

"Earth to Kat," her brother said, handing the phone to her. "It's for you. It's Aunt Jenn."

Kat's favorite daydream in the world ended.

In real life she wasn't allowed to get a puppy.

Her parents said they didn't have enough time to look after puppies.

But she was happy her aunt was phoning her. Aunt Jenn was the best. She loved dogs as much as Kat did. She had opened up a dog-grooming salon in town. Her business was called Tails Up! Boarding and Grooming, and it was doing really well—better than she had thought it would. In fact, Aunt Jenn had just hired someone to help answer the phone and make appointments. But even with her new office helper, Aunt Jenn was still busy, busy, busy. So she often asked Kat to give her a hand. Most times Kat got her best friend, Maya, and her new friend, Grace, to come along. They usually helped Aunt Jenn with puppies that were boarding at Tails Up!

Kat grabbed the phone from Aidan. "Hi, Aunt Jenn!" she said.

"Hi, Kitty-Kat," said Aunt Jenn, using her special name for Kat. "Listen, I wonder if you can help me out. Things are usually busy here on Saturdays. But this morning, there is an extra challenge."

"Sure," said Kat. "What is it? Has someone left a puppy to board with you? Does he need a walk or a play in the yard?"

"Well, something like that—times three!" Aunt Jenn laughed. "This morning I came downstairs to the salon early to prepare for another day of business. I opened the main door to pick up the newspaper, and what did I find? A big cardboard box—with three little white bichon frise puppies in it!" Aunt Jenn said. Now her voice sounded a bit upset.

Kat gasped. "Three abandoned puppies?"

"Yes," Aunt Jenn said. She sighed. "I think they are about eight weeks old. I put them in a kennel in the doggy day care room, and I gave them food and water. They need more attention, but I'm so busy today. It's almost noon, and this is the first chance I've even had to call you. You don't mind helping out this afternoon?"

"Of course not!" Kat said quickly. "Is it okay if Maya and Grace come? We all love helping out at Tails Up! You know how dog crazy we are!"

"That would be wonderful," Aunt Jenn said. "That way there would be three of them and three of you!"

"I'll check with Mom and Dad," said Kat. "Then I'll call Maya and Grace."

"Oh, and, Kitty-Kat, can you bring along poster-making supplies? It would be great if you could make posters advertising that the three pups need homes," suggested Aunt Jenn.

"Sure thing," said Kat. "See you in a flash. Or sooner!"

CHAPTER 2

Fifteen minutes later, Maya and her mom pulled up in front of Kat's house. Maya leaned out the passenger window.

"Hi, Kat-Nip," she called.

Kat made a face. Maya had called her "Kat-Nip" for as long as she could remember. "You love dogs, but your name is Kat? How goofy!" she'd say. Maya often teased her, and Kat teased her back. But it was all in good fun.

They had been best friends forever.

Maya waved Kat over. "I told my mom that

your aunt needs us yesterday," Maya said, grinning, "so she's going to give us a lift to Tails Up!"

Kat jumped into the backseat. "Thanks,
Mrs. Berg."

"You're welcome, Katherine," Maya's mother
answered.

"What about Grace? Is she meeting us there?"
Maya asked as Kat did up her seat belt.

"Yup. In a while," Kat explained, "after a
doctor's appointment. Oh, and she's going to
bring along some art supplies for the posters."

Five minutes later, Maya's mother dropped
off the girls in front of Tails Up! The grooming
salon was on the main street of Orchard Valley,
just a few blocks from Kat's house.

The girls hurried inside. A young man sitting
behind the front desk waved. "Hello, girls,"

he said. "You're Kat? And you're Maya? I'm Tony, the new receptionist," he explained, standing up.

"Hi, Tony," said Maya.

"Nice to meet you," said Kat.

"And this is Marmalade. She's fifteen. She won't go anywhere without me." Tony grinned.

A big, elderly tabby cat was sitting on the countertop.

"Hi, Marmalade," Kat said.

"Can we pet her?" Maya asked.

"Go ahead," Tony said. "But don't think for a moment that she'll enjoy it. She'll allow it but only as a favor to you!" He winked at them.

Kat and Maya stroked the elderly cat, and sure enough, she didn't look at them. But she purred loudly.

The phone rang. "Your aunt should be out in a minute," Tony said, before answering the phone with a cheerful, "Tails Up! How can I help you?"

Kat looked around the waiting room. As always, it was packed. It had a small couch and three chairs. Today, almost every seat was taken. A bald man sat with a stocky bull terrier lying at his feet. A teenage girl with a shaved head, five earrings in one ear, and one in her bottom lip held her Great Dane on a short leash. It had black studs on its collar. It wagged its tail happily at Kat and Maya.

A young woman sat sprawled on a chair. She wore a trim jacket and skirt and black boots. She had long, black hair in tight curls that cascaded down her back.

Maya nudged Kat and tilted her head toward the young woman.

Kat studied her. What breed of dog would she have? This was one of Kat and Maya's favorite games.

"Puli," Kat whispered to Maya after a moment.

"Puli?" Maya frowned. "Okay, Einstein. What's a puli?"

"It's a really rare dog breed," Kat began to explain. "Pulis look really unusual, like moving mops! They have—"

Just then, Aunt Jenn came bounding out of the grooming studio. As usual, her brown hair was pulled back into a ponytail. She wore a light-blue jacket sprinkled with black, brown, tan, and red dog hairs. Beside her bounced a black dog with long cords of tightly curled hair that touched the ground. When he moved, the cords swung back and forth.

"Cocoa!" The young woman bent down to greet her dog. "You good boy!" Her own curls bounced up and down.

"Cocoa's a puli!" Kat said, grinning.

Maya gasped in surprise. "And his owner has a matching hairdo! Nice one, Kat."

Aunt Jenn turned to the waiting clients. "I just need a minute to speak with my niece and her friend. I'll be right back," she said firmly.

"Hello, wonderful girls," she said to Kat and Maya. "Thank you so much for coming!" She waved them to follow her into the doggy day care room.

It had a large fenced-in area, like a playpen. There was a stairway that led to a big room for puppy training and Aunt Jenn's apartment. There was a window looking onto a big fenced-in yard. There were also four large dog kennels along one wall. In the closest one were three little white puppies. When they saw the girls, two of the puppies jumped up and began wagging their tails.

"Here they are," said Aunt Jenn. "The bichon frise pups!"

Kat and Maya squealed with delight and hurried over. They dropped to their knees beside the kennel.

"They are so sweet!" cooed Kat.

"They are so tiny!" exclaimed Maya.

"Two females and one male," Aunt Jenn said, pointing out which was which.

"It's hard to tell them apart," said Maya. "All three are white and so cute!"

"The male looks a little smaller than the females," Kat said thoughtfully. "And he seems a little quieter." The male puppy sat in the corner and watched his sisters play together.

"Likely they are siblings from one litter," said Aunt Jenn. "There may have been others in the litter. Perhaps the owner found homes for the others, but not for these three puppies, and so he or she left them here."

"But why?" Kat said angrily. She stood up.

"Why would anyone just abandon a box of puppies outside a grooming salon?"

"And what if you hadn't found them right away?" Maya added, her eyes flashing. "What if the pups had climbed out of the box and run onto the street?"

"These are good questions," said Aunt Jenn. "We'll never know who put the puppies outside Tails Up! or why. But the good news is that these three little ones are safe and sound!"

"True," Maya said.

Kat nodded. Aunt Jenn was right.

"So your job this afternoon is to play with them while I work." Aunt Jenn stuck her finger in the air. "And also to come up with an action plan. We need to find each one a home—and quickly! These pups are about eight weeks old. They will begin to bond with the people around them. So they need to be with their forever family as soon as possible. We don't want them to bond with us! It would be too difficult for them to separate from us."

Kat swallowed hard. She stared at the puppies. What if they couldn't find homes for all three puppies? What if one pup was left behind and never found his or her forever family?

She forced herself to put the feeling aside. They would just have to do their best to make sure that didn't happen.

You're okay with these three pups? You don't need any reminders on how to lift them out of the kennel or place them back in?" Aunt Jenn asked.

"No, we're fine," said Kat with a smile.

"Good," Aunt Jenn said. She turned to go, but then turned back. "Almost forgot. Names!" she said. "We need to be able to tell the puppies apart when we're talking about them. Can you take care of naming them all?"

Kat paused. "But won't that make them bond with us too much, Aunt Jenn?"

Aunt Jenn shook her head. "Don't think so. Many breeders name their puppies and then the new owners rename them. Puppies learn their new names quickly. I have several books about dogs in my waiting room, including ones filled with names. Help yourself." With one more grin at the girls, she was gone.

Kat's head was swimming. She looked at Maya. "What do we do first?"

Maya slapped her hand to her chest. "Oh, woe is us," she said dramatically. "Decisions, decisions, decisions…"

Kat giggled. Her best friend would make a great actress!

"But seriously, Maya, what do we do first?"

Kat said. She knelt beside the kennel. Two of the puppies tumbled over to her excitedly. Kat longed to play with them all.

"Well, how about we talk about the posters first," said Maya.

Kat turned back to the puppies. "We're going to make posters to tell people about you three," she told them. The two puppies wagged their tails excitedly. The third pup stayed in the corner, just watching.

"We'll put up posters around town, and we can put them up at school on Monday as well," said Maya.

"Okay," said Kat. "We'll write on the posters that these puppies will only go to responsible people. People who will take good care of them and love them forever."

"Sounds good," Maya agreed. "Now, while we wait for Grace to come with the poster supplies, why don't we play with the pups?"

"Great idea!" said Kat.

Maya hurried over to join Kat by the crate.

"The male is a little smaller, but the two females are exactly the same size," Maya said, looking at the puppies. "Spunky and lively. White with black noses and black button eyes. It's hard to tell them apart."

Kat looked back and forth, back and forth at the females. "You're right," she agreed. "Identical."

"You know what?" Maya said, looking at them closely. "I think there is one difference, after all. Neither of them actually has black eyes. She has eyes that are almost black." She pointed to the pup on the left. "But *her* eyes are dark brown!"

Kat peered at the puppies, then smiled. "You're right, Maya!"

Kat opened the kennel and reached in. The two females came right over. They looked up at Kat and licked her fingers happily.

"Okay, you first, little one," Kat said. Gently she lifted up the puppy with the almost-black eyes. She hugged the squirming puffball against her chest.

"You are adorable," Kat said softly. "Just adorable."

She stroked the puppy's soft coat. She liked how her tail curled up over her back, just like the top of a question mark.

Maya lifted out the other female puppy.

"Oh, she is so tiny!" Maya said. "I don't think I've ever held such a little puppy!"

"It's almost like holding a stuffed toy dog, isn't it?" Kat exclaimed. "Except these puppies are real!"

Kat cuddled the puppy for a few more minutes. Then she set her down. "Time to play!" At once the curious female began to explore the room. She sniffed the three other kennels, which were empty. She found a basket of dog toys. She pulled out a plush squirrel. She held it between her teeth and shook her head from side to side.

Kat laughed. "The squirrel is almost as big as the puppy!"

Maya set the other puppy down. She ran to join her sister. The two bichon frise pups began to play a happy game of tug-of-war.

Kat looked at the male puppy. He still sat

in the corner of the kennel. He was watching his sisters closely. He didn't look nervous or scared, just cautious.

"Your turn to come out," Kat told him. She put her hand in the kennel. The puppy approached it slowly. He sniffed Kat's hand. Then, quick as a wink, out came his pink tongue to give her hand a gentle lick.

"Thank you," said Kat, feeling especially pleased. "Nice to meet you too. Now here we go," she said and picked him up. He was so soft. Kat held the puppy close against her chest. She could feel his heart thumping. He was even tinier than his sisters.

Suddenly Kat was worried. The puppies were very sweet, but it might be difficult to find owners for all three. Especially in only a few days. Especially if one puppy acted a little shy. What would happen if they couldn't find someone who would love each puppy forever? What would happen to this little fellow if they couldn't find someone who wanted to take him home?

CHAPTER 4

The door opened, and Grace peeked her head in.

"Kat? Maya?" she called.

"Hi, Grace," replied Kat. "Come in quickly and close the door behind you. The puppies are loose!"

Grace quickly slipped into the room. "Hi, guys! Sorry I'm late," she said. Grace caught sight of the three puppies. "Oh my goodness!" she cooed. She whipped off her backpack and dropped the art supplies by the door. "Look at you cute little things!"

Kat remembered the first time she saw Grace. It was just a short time ago. Grace had just moved to Orchard Valley. She was put in Kat's class. She stood at the front of the room with their teacher, Ms. Mitchell. She didn't smile. Her arms were straight down at her sides. Her face was stony.

At first Kat thought Grace was just…mean. That's what all the other kids in the class thought too. But Kat had been helping Aunt Jenn look after a puppy called Riley. And Riley had taught her that Grace was just missing her own dog and her own home. Grace looked mean when she was scared or embarrassed.

Now Grace squatted on the floor. The two female pups were chasing a ball across the floor. But when they saw the girl crouching there, they hurried over to her, their legs flying. They jumped up at her like jack-in-the-boxes.

"Bichons are really great at doing tricks. In the past they performed in circuses," said Kat, grinning.

Kat read about dogs on the Internet. She read every dog book she could get her hands on. Her favorite book was *Dog Breeds of the World.* She must have read it more than twenty times. She wanted to learn everything she could about dogs.

Grace clapped her hands together. "I can't believe it! Just look at these two prance and pirouette!" She patted one puppy with each hand. "Hello, my friends!" Then she looked at the male puppy. "And what about this little one?" He was happily chewing on a squeaky toy. "Come on over and see me," Grace coaxed. "Come on." She stretched out a hand to the puppy. He wagged his tail, but he stayed where he was. His sisters jumped at Grace's hand, wanting the attention back on them.

"So, first things first," said take-charge Maya. "Grace, we have to find names for these three. I'll get the books Aunt Jenn mentioned."

Maya hurried out to the waiting room and returned with the books. She passed them out. Then she pulled out some paper and a pen from the bag of art supplies.

"I'll be the recorder," Maya said. "Okay, anytime you find a good name, call it out, and I'll write it down."

The girls settled into a brainstorming session. Kat sat on the floor near the male puppy. She found a section in her book on names for male dogs. As she looked through the names, she tugged on the squeaky toy. The puppy pulled back on the toy, his head down and his rear end up in the air. She liked his fierce little growling sounds.

"How about Snowball?" suggested Grace. She flicked the end of one of her long red braids. "Or Snowflake?"

"Good. I'll write those down," said Maya.

"Puff?" Grace added.

"You know," said Kat thoughtfully, "the name *bichon frise* is French, and it actually means *curly lap dog*."

"Perfect!" Grace laughed. "I bet I could fit both of these pups in my lap at once!"

"So, maybe it would be a good idea to give these puppies French names," suggested Kat.

"Mais oui!" cried Maya. "That's a great idea!"

Grace smiled, but it was difficult for Kat to tell if she agreed or not. She didn't often tell the girls what she was thinking. *Grace is a little like the third bichon frise puppy*, Kat thought with a grin. *A bit quiet. A bit cautious.*

Kat wondered if Grace was like that with everyone. Or was it just with her and Maya? Kat had become friends with Grace first. Then she had introduced her to Maya. The two of them were getting along all right now, but the other kids at school still didn't seem to know what to make of Grace. Kat hoped Grace would make more new friends soon.

She sighed. For some reason, friendship was definitely not easy. And sometimes kids at school seemed to make things even harder.

Dogs seem to make friends a lot easier than people do, Kat thought.

Just then, the male puppy picked up the squeaky toy and trotted to the other side of the room. He flopped down and curled up with the toy, all alone.

Except for this guy, that is, Kat thought. *He doesn't seem to want to make friends with us!*

"So come on, girls," Maya said impatiently. "Names! We need names! And in French, *si'l vous plaît*!" Maya made googly eyes. "That means *please*, for those who don't understand French as well as *moi*!"

Kat and Grace giggled. Soon the names were flying. Maya listed them all.

While the girls worked, the two female puppies fell asleep near the basket of toys—one on top of the other, exhausted from their exploring, running, and tugging. The male puppy snoozed, tucked up against his squeaky toy.

"Okay," announced Maya after a while. "I think we have a long enough list."

Maya read out the names one by one, and the girls voted for the names they liked best. Grace jotted down the scores.

"Now for the results," said Maya after doing a tally. "First, the female with the deep, dark eyes. She will be Aimée, which means *loved*. The female with the chocolate-brown eyes is Chantal. I don't know what it means, but it sounds so pretty. *Chantal, Chantal!*" repeated Maya, grinning. "And the male? Say *bonjour* to Bijou, which means *jewel*."

"Perfect," said Grace. "I love these names."

"Me too." Kat smiled, delighted.

CHAPTER 5

Grace pulled out the markers, pens, paper, and poster boards. The girls talked about what to write on the posters so they could find good homes for the puppies.

"Must be kind and loving," suggested Maya.

"Must be willing to go on walks—rain or snow," said Grace.

"Must need a very special friend," added Kat, looking at Bijou.

Then, all at once the puppies woke up. Right away, they were on the go! Chantal scooted to the corner of the room and peed. With a happy yip, Aimée pounced on a marker that had fallen to the floor. And Bijou decided to try to chew open a bag of dog biscuits that Aunt Jenn had set by the back door.

The girls decided to take turns playing with the puppies and making the posters. As they worked, Aunt Jenn came into the doggy day care room.

"How's it going in here?" Aunt Jenn asked. She popped a piece of gum in her mouth. "How are the little ones?"

"We've named the puppies Aimée, Chantal, and Bijou," explained Kat. "We're making posters, and we're going to post them up and down the main street and at school!"

"Wonderful!" exclaimed Aunt Jenn. "Please

put the Tails Up! telephone number on the posters. Tony can arrange for us to meet with any interested callers."

She grinned as Aimée and Chantal came tumbling toward her. "I hope there are three families out there who want new puppies—and soon! These scallywags really need to be with their own people soon."

Aunt Jenn squatted down. The two fluffy white puppies covered her hand in kisses. "But I'm sure we won't have any trouble once they meet them. These two certainly are hard to resist!" She laughed.

Kat looked at Bijou, who was sitting watching his sisters. He had his head cocked to one side. *What about him?* Kat wondered. *Will Bijou be friendly enough to get a family of his own?*

It gave her a funny feeling. Part of her wanted the puppy to be left behind. Maybe she could convince her parents to let her bring him home! But another part of her knew that wasn't possible. And if no one wanted him, what would happen to the sweet little guy?

Kat shuddered and put the thought out of her head.

"I must get back to my clients," said Aunt Jenn, standing up again. "Now, girls, when you leave, please make sure the puppies are safely back in their kennel." Aunt Jenn blew a pink bubble with her gum. "Also, Kitty-Kat, could you, Maya, and Grace come after school on Monday and help out with these three again? That is, if they're all still here."

"Sure," said Kat. She looked at Maya and Grace, who both nodded enthusiastically.

"Lovely. Well then, ta-ta!" Aunt Jenn said cheerily. And off she went.

CHAPTER 6

All morning and all afternoon, Kat couldn't stop thinking about Bijou. She sat in class at her desk with her math questions in front of her. But she didn't see numbers. Instead she saw a cute little white bichon frise chewing on a squeaky toy. She saw him cuddled up across the room, sleeping. She saw him looking at her, his head cocked to one side, cautious.

Kat looked at the clock. She sighed. The hands did not seem to be moving very quickly today.

Come on, she told herself. *Just focus. Do your assignment. It might make the time go by faster.*

She bent over her math questions and began to work.

When she looked up again, the hands on the clock had moved. Finally.

Kat grinned and looked at Grace, who sat at the desk beside her. Grace was pulling at one of her braids and staring into space. Her paper was blank.

"Hey," Kat whispered. "I know what you're thinking about."

Grace smiled back at her.

"Bichon frise puppies? And the interviews?"

Grace nodded.

"All right, class," said Ms. Mitchell. She stood at the front of the room. Behind her, on the blackboard, she had written the same math questions that were on their papers. "Now, I need some brave souls to come up and show us their work. But I'm not going to ask for volunteers this time." She looked around. "Owen, Cora, Lindsay, Grace. Come up, please."

Grace shot Kat a panicked look. She didn't move from her seat while the other children got up and went to the board.

"Grace, you have to go," Kat told her. She gave her shoulder a gentle push.

"I can't do it," Grace said. She flushed.

"That's okay. Just go and try," Kat suggested.

"I'll get them all wrong," Grace said.

"Ms. Mitchell will help you," Kat told her.

Someone snickered from behind. It was Megan. She sat behind Grace.

Kat turned around and glared at Megan. Megan rolled her eyes, like she thought Grace was stupid. It wasn't the first time. Megan had been mean to Grace from the start.

Kat decided not to say anything. It might just encourage Megan. That's what Kat's mom said sometimes when she was arguing with Aidan. Megan snickered again, and Grace must have heard her. Grace had that mean look on her face. Her face looked like stone. Kat knew it meant Grace was embarrassed or uncomfortable. It didn't mean she was going to do something nasty. It didn't even mean she was thinking unpleasant thoughts. That was the thing you had to know about Grace. How she looked didn't often equal how she felt. It wasn't like a math question.

Grace got up and began walking to the board.

"The new girl. What's her name again?" Megan said, pretending she'd forgotten. She spoke just loud enough so Kat and Grace could hear.

Grace kept walking. Her arms were straight down at her sides.

She picked up the chalk and looked at

the math questions, but she didn't write anything.

Just as Kat had predicted, Ms. Mitchell came and stood beside her. She talked to Grace in a soft voice, pointing at the numbers, explaining what to do. In only a few minutes, Grace was filling in all the answers and they were correct.

When the end-of-the-day bell rang, Kat and Grace hurried out to meet Maya.

"That Megan is so mean," Kat said to Grace.

Grace didn't reply.

"I should say something to her. Defend you," suggested Kat. "Tell Ms. Mitchell she's bothering you. Or...do something mean to her. Take revenge. That's what Maya always says, and maybe she's right..." Kat didn't like the idea, but maybe it would work.

"No!" Grace said. She turned to Kat and put her hand on her arm, stopping her. "No. Don't."

"But…" Kat stopped. She could see tears in Grace's eyes.

"Don't. Please," Grace insisted.

"Okay," agreed Kat. "I won't."

♡ ✬ ◎

Maya was waiting at the usual spot.

"So?" she asked, as they headed down the street toward the grooming salon. "Let's have it. Joke of the day. You forgot to tell us one this morning before school."

Grace slapped her forehead and tried not to grin. "And I thought I'd escaped."

"No, it is a tradition that we must endure," said Maya. "Come on now, Kat-Nip. Hit us with one."

Kat thought for a moment. "What do you get if you cross a sheepdog with a rose?" she asked.

"I don't know," said Maya.

"Me neither," said Grace.

"A cauliflower!" cried Kat. "Get it? A collie-flower?"

"Oh! So bad," moaned Maya.

"So, so bad," echoed Grace. "Worst ever."

Kat started to laugh. But just then Megan and Cora rode by on their bikes.

"Kat and Owen sitting in a tree," they chant-ed. "K-I-S-S-I-N-G."

The two girls didn't even look at Kat. But

Kat knew they meant her to hear them. That Megan. Take the *g* out of her name and it spelled *mean*.

Maya frowned. "I thought they stopped teasing you after you stood up to them," she said to Kat.

"Yeah, well, they started again," Kat said. She shrugged. She tried to pretend it didn't bother her. She hoped they weren't teasing Owen too. He wasn't her boyfriend, but he was nice.

Soon the girls reached Aunt Jenn's salon. Inside it was as crowded as usual. Tony looked up, gave a friendly wave, and then went back to typing on the computer. Marmalade stuck her tail up in the air and pretended the girls weren't there.

Kat stroked Marmalade's back anyway. "You can't fool me," she whispered into the tabby cat's ear.

Then Kat led Maya and Grace past the five clients: a border collie, two Pomeranians, a West Highland terrier, and a Doberman.

Kat paused with her hand on the door to the doggy day care room. What if one or two of the puppies were gone? What if Bijou wasn't there?

CHAPTER 7

Kat breathed a sigh of relief. All three of the puppies were still there. Kat wanted the puppies to find homes, but she didn't want them to leave without saying good-bye! And of course Aunt Jenn wouldn't let that happen. Not even if the puppies did find homes.

The girls put down their backpacks and hurried over to the kennel.

"Hello, Chantal. *Bonjour!*" said Maya, lifting out the brown-eyed puppy. Chantal licked Maya's cheeks and wiggled with excitement.

"Now you, Aimée. Out you come," said Grace. She gave the snow-white puppy a quick kiss on her tiny head.

"And you too, Bijou," murmured Kat. The puppy wagged his curled-up tail while she held him close. He was being so friendly. Maybe he remembered her! Kat smelled his lovely puppy smell. She stroked his soft coat.

"Play time!" announced Kat. When the girls set down the puppies, Chantal and Aimée scampered toward each other and began to wrestle. Bijou, however, had other things on his mind. He headed over to the toy basket and found a small plastic ball. He tried to bite it, but it was much too large for him to get a grip. It rolled away, and he chased it and tried again.

"Those sisters are going to miss each other,"

said Maya, watching them tussle. "But this one?" Maya added, pointing to Bijou. "Not so much. He's a bit of a loner, isn't he?"

The time went quickly. The girls knew they had to make the most of it. Perhaps all the puppies would have new homes by tomorrow!

Maya and Grace played with Aimée and Chantal. They sat on the floor across from each other with the puppies in between them. They rolled a soccer ball back and forth to each other. The puppies ran back and forth too, chasing the ball. A few times, Chantal was so excited she almost did a somersault. Aimée kept skidding into the girls' legs, unable to stop in time.

Bijou seemed happy playing alone, but Kat was worried. "You need to be able to socialize," she whispered to him. "It's important. Most people get dogs because they want to play with them. You won't get chosen if you don't seem very friendly."

Kat took Bijou's ball and threw it for him, but he wouldn't chase it.

He headed back to the toy basket and picked out a toy bone. He growled and shook it in his mouth.

Kat laughed. "Here, bring it here!" she said, crouching down and patting the floor. "Bring it to me!" But Bijou didn't come. He didn't even look at her.

Kat got a real dog biscuit from the bag that was now up on the shelf. She sat down across from Bijou.

"Look, Bijou! A biscuit for you!" she said, trying to tempt him. "Come here. Come here and you can have it."

Bijou dropped the toy bone.

"Here you go. Good puppy!" Kat said encouragingly.

Bijou turned and went back to the toy basket to look for another toy.

Kat looked at Maya and Grace. They were both lying on their backs giggling, and Chantal and Aimée were climbing up and over them.

"Your little paws are as light as feathers, Chantal!" giggled Maya.

"Oh, that tickles!" squealed Grace, as Aimée scampered across her tummy.

Kat sighed. Bijou had found a new toy and was happily chewing on it, all by himself.

Suddenly Maya cried out, "Oh! I almost forgot!" She gently pushed Chantal off her stomach and got up. "I brought my camera!" She went to her backpack and took it out.

"Good!" said Kat, jumping up as well. "We

can add Chantal, Aimée, and Bijou to our Puppy Collection!"

Maya began snapping photos of Chantal, who was trying to spring up onto Grace's belly. Then Grace sat up and set Aimée on the floor. Maya took photos of the puppy as she yipped and chased her sister, Chantal, across the room.

"These photos will be perfect for the Puppy Collection," Grace said.

Maya and Kat had started the Puppy Collection together just a short time ago. Neither girl was allowed to have a dog, so they did the next best thing. They drew pictures of their favorite puppies or they took photos of them. They gave each puppy a name and wrote a description of it. They also added puppies they met, such as the ones they helped to look after at Tails Up! Now that Grace was their friend, she helped with the Puppy Collection too.

"Don't forget to take some photos of Bijou," Kat reminded Maya.

"Why don't you pick him up?" suggested Maya. "I'll take one of both of you."

Kat was happy to scoop up the puppy. But when she tried to get him to look at the camera, he only wanted to gaze at her quietly with his dark-brown button eyes. She looked back at him, her heart melting.

A while later, it was time to go. The girls put the puppies back in the kennel and said good night to them. They grabbed their backpacks and closed the door to the doggy day care behind them.

Just then Aunt Jenn came hurrying down the hall.

"Ah, good. You're still here! Can't chat long. I still have two more dogs to groom." She pulled out her ponytail and made a new one. "But I wanted to tell you that I've set up an interview with someone interested in adopting one of our puppies. Would you girls be able to come and sit in on it? It's tomorrow after school."

Kat's heart sank, but she knew it was a good thing. The puppies needed their own homes as soon as possible.

"Sure thing," said Kat firmly. "I can come."

"Not me," Maya said. She made a face. "I have my piano lesson tomorrow."

"I'll be here." Grace nodded enthusiastically. "I can help."

"Thank you," said Aunt Jenn. She flashed them a smile. "See you tomorrow, then. And now, I'm off!"

CHAPTER 8

School was over for the day. Kat stood in the school entranceway waiting for Grace. Kat was looking at one of the posters they had put up the previous morning. *What's going to happen after school today?* Kat wondered. Three puppies but only one interview.

"Tails Up! Um…isn't that your aunt's boarding and grooming place?"

Kat jumped. She hadn't noticed that Owen was standing beside her reading the poster. She had been daydreaming again.

"Yes," she said.

He blushed. She didn't know why.

"Does she let me...you, I mean..." He frowned. He took a breath. "Does she let you come and pay...I mean, play with the dogs sometimes?" he asked.

Kat tried not to smile. "Yes, she does," she told him.

Maya was certain Owen got tongue-tied around Kat because he liked her. Megan and Cora thought so too. A short time ago, they had teased Kat about it and even written her a note with hearts on it. *Dreaming about Owen?* Of course Kat had been daydreaming about puppies, not Owen. Owen was her friend, not her boyfriend. Kat didn't mind Maya teasing her, but it wasn't okay for Megan and Cora to do it. They were trying to annoy her. They only stopped when they thought she was going to show their note to Ms. Mitchell. They didn't want to get in trouble with their teacher.

They aren't picking on me as much as they used to. But Megan seems to be teasing Grace more than ever, Kat thought, remembering how Megan had acted yesterday. *And today she pretended to forget Grace's name again. Which is just plain mean.*

"That must be fun," said Owen.

Kat looked at him blankly. Megan, being teased…

"Playing with the dogs. At Tails Up!" Owen added.

"Oh, yes. Yes, it is!" Kat said hastily. "In fact, I'm waiting for Grace and then we're going there. To Tails Up! Ms. Mitchell wanted to speak to her first."

Owen nodded. He wasn't looking at Kat anymore. He was looking at the poster. He didn't speak for a moment. *Had he run out of things to say?* Kat wondered.

"You seem to love dogs so much," Owen said. When he said the word *love*, he blushed again.

Kat didn't know why, but she blushed too. "I do," Kat agreed. "Love dogs, I mean." She felt stupid for blushing. What was wrong with her?

Then Sunjit called out from down the hall, "O-wen. Come on, O. We're heading out." He was bouncing a basketball.

Thank goodness. Kat had never felt so awkward. Especially with a friend.

"Well, bye," said Owen. He put on his hat with the earflaps. He wore it all the time.

Kat grinned. She and Maya thought it made Owen look like a basset hound!

"See you," said Kat.

Owen stood for a moment without moving.

"O-wen. Come on!" yelled Sunjit.

"Bye," said Owen again. He headed down the hall toward his friend.

Just then Grace appeared.

"Sorry about that!" she said breathlessly. "Ms. Mitchell made some math sheets for me. She wanted to go over a few problems with me too." Grace put on her backpack.

"Did you tell Ms. Mitchell about Megan? That she's been mean to you?" asked Kat as they headed outside.

"No." Grace shook her head. "But I think she noticed yesterday, when I went up to the board to do the math problems. She asked me if I wanted her to talk to Megan."

"Oh, that's great," said Kat with relief. "That'll show Megan that she can't treat you that way."

Grace shrugged. "Well, not really."

"What do you mean?" Kat asked.

"I said no. I said I would work it out myself," Grace said.

Kat stared at her. "You're kidding," she said.

"No," Grace said. "I know it's good to tell an adult when you're having problems, but…I don't know. I think it's better for me to do this on my own."

"Well, it's important to stand up for yourself," Kat said slowly. She knew from firsthand experience how hard that could be.

The girls left the schoolyard and headed down the street. "Maybe Megan's just not very self-confident and she's mean to me to make herself feel better," said Grace.

Kat was impressed. "Maybe," she said.

"In any case, don't worry," said Grace. "I'm sure I'll be able to work it out. Somehow."

"Okay. Just let me know if I can help." Kat grinned. "But in the meantime, the puppies are waiting."

"And the interview will start soon!" added Grace.

Kat pulled Grace's arm. "Come on, slow-poke! Let's run. Last one to Tails Up! is a rotten tomato!"

CHAPTER 9

Here he is. Kat, Grace, meet Bill Bracer. He's come to speak with us about our bichon frise puppies," said Aunt Jenn. She led the man into the doggy day care room.

"Hello, girls," said Bill Bracer. He had snow-white hair and a bushy white beard. His back was a little stooped, and he walked with a cane. He had a big smile. But when he saw the three puppies in the kennel, his smile grew even bigger. "Well, aren't they something!" he said.

Mr. Bracer went right over and looked in at the puppies. He put his fingers through one of the openings. Aimée and Chantal wiggled and wagged. They poked their little noses at him. Bijou sat to the side and watched, curious.

"Would you like to hold one of the puppies?" Aunt Jenn asked. She nodded to Kat.

"This one is a girl. Her name is Chantal," Kat told Mr. Bracer, pointing. "This is Chantal's sister. Her name is Aimée." Then she pointed toward Bijou. "And this is Bijou, the only boy."

Kat watched closely. Mr. Bracer smiled, but he didn't even seem to look at Bijou.

"Bijou is quiet, but he's sweet," Kat added quickly. She couldn't help it.

"Well, I'm sure he is, but I do so like the look of this little pup here," Mr. Bracer said, pointing to Aimée. "Seems awfully friendly. Could I please hold her?"

Aunt Jenn nodded. Kat picked up Aimée and handed her to Mr. Bracer. He hung his cane on his arm and took the puppy carefully, pulling her close to his chest.

"Oh my. You are lovely, Aimée," he said. "A sweet little handful of fluff!" Mr. Bracer looked into the kennel again. "That other little brown-eyed gal looks very sweet as well," he said. "May I hold her too?"

Kat looked at Aunt Jenn, who nodded. She picked up Chantal and handed her to Mr. Bracer.

Kat grinned as the puppies wiggled happily, licking each other's faces.

"These sisters are good pals," said Mr. Bracer jovially. "They remind me of my last pair of dogs. They were sisters too. Pugs. One never went anywhere without the other! Well, Aimée and Chantal, wouldn't it be nice if I could take you both home with me?"

Grace nudged Kat and lifted her eyebrows. "Both puppies?" she whispered. "He wants both!"

Kat nodded, excited. "Wouldn't that be great?" she whispered back.

Aunt Jenn cleared her throat. "So, Mr. Bracer," she said, her voice solemn. "You've answered all my questions already, but Grace and Kat have a few more questions they'd like to ask you, if that's all right."

"Oh my, my, yes. I bet they have something to do with what it said on the poster, correct?" Mr. Bracer said.

He looked at Kat and Grace. "So here are your answers, girls. I memorized all the points. They were that important to me." He winked at them. "Kind and loving? You bet. Willing to go on walks? Rain or snow? Indeedy. Need a very special friend? I should say so." He hugged Aimée and Chantal close. "You can count on me being a fine owner to these little gals. I'll treat them like princesses. I promise."

Kat couldn't help but think about Bijou. "Mr. Bracer, wouldn't you like to take Bijou as well? The girls might be lonely without their brother, and Bijou…well, he's quiet, but he'll grow on you, I know it!" she said.

The white-haired man shook his head. "If I didn't have this cane, I might consider it, young lady," he said gently. "But I think these two are really all I can handle."

Kat, Grace, and Aunt Jenn had a quick, private meeting. All of them agreed that Mr. Bracer would be a wonderful owner for Aimée and Chantal.

Aunt Jenn handed Mr. Bracer a list of puppy instructions and a kit of doggy items that she had prepared. Tony helped carry the two puppies out to Mr. Bracer's car.

"I will certainly bring these gals back to visit you kind folks," Mr. Bracer said. "That's a promise too."

Kat smiled back at him. She was sorry Bijou wasn't going along. But this was certainly a perfect match. Aimée and Chantal were in good hands.

After Mr. Bracer left, Kat and Grace played with Bijou together. They sat on the floor across from each other and rolled a ball between them. Bijou ran back and forth, chasing the ball. Kat and Grace laughed as the little puppy tried to pick up the ball.

"It's too big," Kat told him. "And your mouth is just too small!"

After a while, Grace sighed. "I have to go home early," she said. "I promised my mom I'd work on my math homework before dinner."

She said good-bye to Bijou and Kat.

Kat was a little bit pleased. She liked having some time alone with Bijou. She picked up the puppy and cuddled him. She played tug-of-war with him. She practiced "sit" with him, giving him a little piece of dog biscuit when he followed her command.

She felt sad putting him back in the empty kennel. "Will you miss your sisters?" she asked.

But Bijou didn't look unhappy. He curled up in a corner of the kennel, wagged his tail twice, and then closed his eyes.

For a while Kat just stood and looked at him.

She worried Bijou might not win anyone's heart but hers. Today, for example, Mr. Bracer had poked his fingers in the crate and said hello to the puppies. But Bijou hadn't come over like his sisters had.

Of course, not all puppies were the same. Just like people.

Kat thought about Maya. She was like Aimée and Chantal—enthusiastic and eager from the get-go. Grace was more like Bijou—neither of them jumped into things. It didn't mean they didn't like to have fun. It didn't mean they weren't friendly. They just took their time to show it.

"Bye, Bijou," Kat whispered to the sleeping pup. "I really hope someone will show up here who will love you as much as I do!"

CHAPTER 10

On Wednesday and again on Thursday, Kat, Grace, and Maya went to Tails Up! after school. They played ball with Bijou. Kat spent more time teaching him to sit on command.

Each day Aunt Jenn told them that several people had called about the abandoned bichon frise puppies, but none of them were the best fit for Bijou.

Kat was getting more and more worried.

But when Kat, Maya, and Grace arrived at

Tails Up! on Friday, Aunt Jenn had a smile on her face. "Good news! A family is coming this afternoon to see Bijou," she told them. "Let's keep our fingers crossed that this is a good match! I'll bring them into the doggy day care room when they arrive."

"Oh, phew!" breathed Maya with relief. She slapped her hand to her chest dramatically. "Now Bijou's self-esteem won't be shattered for all time!"

"Maya!" protested Kat. But she couldn't stop grinning.

A family was coming to see Bijou! A family who had passed Aunt Jenn's phone inspection. This was the puppy's big chance!

The girls went into the doggy day care room. Kat went to the kennel. When Bijou saw her, he wagged his tail. But he stayed sitting in the corner as always.

"Oh, Bijou," Kat said, picking him up. "You are so calm and quiet. You are a very special puppy!"

"I hope the family coming today can see that!" Maya said.

Kat cuddled the puppy and then set him down. "This might be the last time we get to play with you," she told him. "So let's have fun!"

Grace dangled a knotted rope toy in front of Bijou, then she threw it across the room. "Here you go, Bijou! Go get it!"

The girls played with the puppy for about an hour. Kat felt happy and sad at the same time—happy that Bijou might get a new home, sad that she might not be able to see him again. She kept looking at the time. She kept waiting for the day care room door to open.

Then finally it did.

"This is where we keep our boarders," Aunt

Jenn was saying. "And this is where we are keeping Bijou right now."

Kat scooped up Bijou so he wouldn't try to run into the hallway. Then she turned to look at the new family. Her mouth dropped open. Then she frowned.

No. No way.

CHAPTER 11

Aunt Jenn smiled at the girls. "Kat, Grace, Maya, meet Mr. and Mrs. Fernandez and their daughter Megan."

"Hello," said Maya. "Nice to meet you."

Kat and Grace were too surprised to speak. Megan! It was Megan.

They stared at their classmate. Then they looked at each other. Megan squirmed uncomfortably.

Maya shot Kat a puzzled look, sensing something was going on.

"Do you girls know one another?" Aunt Jenn said, noticing the silence.

"We…we're in the same class," said Megan. She gave a little wave. "Hey, Kat. Grace."

Still the girls didn't speak. But Aunt Jenn continued on with her introductions. "And this," she said, pointing toward the puppy in Kat's arms, "is Bijou."

"Oh, he's so sweet," said Megan. She clasped her hands together. "Look at him, Mom and Dad. Isn't he sweet?"

"Yes, he sure is," agreed Megan's mother.

Megan's father smiled happily and nodded.

Megan came toward Kat, as if Bijou were a magnet. Her eyes were glued to the white bichon frise puppy.

"Hello there, Bijou," she said gently. "Oh, you're adorable!"

"Kat," said Aunt Jenn. "Can you let Megan hold him?"

Kat glared at Megan, but Megan didn't even notice. Kat wanted to say no. She wanted to tell Megan that she couldn't have Bijou, even for a moment.

"Kat?" Aunt Jenn repeated.

Grace nodded at her to follow Aunt Jenn's instructions.

Carefully, Kat handed the puppy to Megan.

Bijou went very still in Megan's arms. He didn't try to kiss her. He didn't wag his tail.

But Megan didn't seem to mind. She held Bijou nicely. She rubbed his ears, just the way he liked it. She kissed his little nose.

"He's perfect," said Megan, her voice trembling. "Just perfect."

Next Mr. and Mrs. Fernandez took turns holding Bijou. Then they set down the puppy. He ran to Kat and hid behind her legs.

"That's okay," said Megan to her parents. "He just needs to get used to us."

Megan sat on the floor near Kat. Quietly she held out her hand. "Here, Bijou," she called. "Come and say hello when you're ready."

Kat wanted to scoop Bijou up and hug him, but instead she waited to see what he would do. She had to give Megan a chance. For Bijou's sake. And in a few minutes, Bijou did go over to Megan. He sniffed her hand and then licked it. In a moment, he climbed right up into her lap and made himself comfortable.

Megan's parents were speaking to each other. Then Mr. Fernandez turned and said, "We would very much like to take Bijou home with us. We would like him to be our very own puppy, if it's all right with you."

Aunt Jenn smiled. "Very good," she said. "You've answered all my questions already on the phone. It's up to Grace, Maya, and Kat now."

Megan looked down at Bijou. She stroked the puppy's head. She was clearly uncomfortable.

Kat wanted to ask, "How can we give you a puppy when we don't think you're a nice person? Will you stop teasing me about Owen? Will you stop teasing Grace too?"

But she decided not to. Grace had told Kat that she wanted to work it out with Megan on her own. So Kat would leave it to Grace. This was her big chance. Now Megan could see how it felt when people were mean. Kat turned to Grace and nodded encouragingly.

Megan looked worried. She was biting her lip. She held Bijou close.

Grace fixed Megan in a stare. But all Grace said was, "Megan. Do you promise to be loving to Bijou? Do you promise to be kind?"

Megan kissed Bijou on the top of his little white head. She took a breath and looked right

into Grace's eyes. Megan's voice shook a little. "Yes, I'll be loving. I'll be kind. I promise." She looked at Grace and Kat. "I know I'm not always the nicest person in the world. But I promise to be Bijou's very best friend. I will take very, very good care of him."

If Megan wasn't teasing everyone all the time, Kat thought, *I might even believe her. She sounds like she means it.*

For a long moment, Grace and Megan just looked at each other.

Kat waited. What was Grace going to say? This was her chance to make Megan sorry for the way she had treated her.

But Grace didn't say anything. And then Aunt Jenn was saying cheerfully, "All right then, Fernandez family. We'll just leave you for a moment with Bijou. Kat, Grace, Maya, and I need to have a quick meeting. Then we'll tell you our decision."

Kat followed her two friends and Aunt Jenn into the hallway.

"So, what do you think, girls?" Aunt Jenn asked. She pumped her fist into the air once, twice. "Perfect, right?"

Maya nodded. "They get my vote," she said.

"I think they will give our sweet little Bijou a good home," agreed Aunt Jenn. "Kat? Grace? You two agree?"

Kat looked at Grace. But Grace was deep in thought.

"Grace?" Aunt Jenn asked.

Kat nudged Grace. "Go on," she whispered. "Tell her."

Grace shook her head.

"What is it?" Aunt Jenn asked. "Is there something I should know? Kat?"

Grace shook her head again at Kat, like a warning.

"No," Grace said quickly. "There's nothing. And yes." Suddenly she smiled. "Yes, I think Megan and her family will give Bijou a good home." She nodded. "And you do too, don't you, Kat?"

Kat stared at her friend. "You're sure?" she asked.

"Yup. I'm sure," Grace said firmly. Kat was surprised. But it was up to Grace. And even though Grace didn't always seem like the most self-confident girl in the world, Kat had confidence in her.

When they went back inside and told the Fernandez family the news, Kat saw Megan's face light up.

"Thank you," she said to Aunt Jenn and Maya.

Megan approached Kat and Grace. "Thank you," she said to the two girls. "Very much." She hugged Bijou close. Her voice was shaky again. "I never thought I'd be able to have my own puppy, especially one as sweet as Bijou."

Kat sighed with relief. Bijou had a home and a best friend. And Megan actually seemed like she would take really good care of him.

Maybe this girl is different than she seems on the outside. Just like another girl I know,

Kat thought, thinking of Grace. She grinned. *And just like a sweet little bichon frise puppy I know*, Kat thought, thinking, of course, of Bijou himself.

CHAPTER 12

Maya, Grace, and Kat sat on the floor of Kat's bedroom.

Grace was sticking photos of the bichon frise puppies into the Puppy Collection scrapbook. Kat was drawing a picture of them.

"How's this?" Maya stuck the pencil behind her ear and read aloud: "Chantal, Aimée, and Bijou are bichon frises. They are two months old. Chantal and Aimée are sisters. They are lively and outgoing. They like to be together! Bijou is their brother. He likes to take his time getting to know people. He is quiet and very sweet."

"Nice," said Kat. "Just right."

"So, which of you is going to tell me what was going on this afternoon?" Maya asked. She raised her eyebrows.

Kat looked at Grace.

"Go ahead," Grace said, grinning.

So Kat told Maya the whole story. "That was *your* Megan?" Maya asked. "Megan from your class?" Maya's mouth dropped open as she listened. She knew Megan had been mean to Kat, but she didn't know Megan had been mean to Grace too.

"She's so annoying," said Maya, shaking her head. "I can't believe you both agreed to give her Bijou! You could have told Aunt Jenn that

Megan was mean. She'd never have given Bijou to her."

Grace grinned. "Yeah, I know," she agreed. "But I thought we should give her a chance. Not just judge her because of the way she is to us. She was able to see right through to the sweetness inside Bijou. I thought we should try to do the same for her. I have a feeling she'll be wonderful with this puppy."

"Maybe," Maya said slowly. "Maybe you're right."

But Kat said firmly, "Well, I know you are. Good call, Grace."

Grace began to blush. So Kat quickly said, "And now, you lucky, lucky friends, I have a special treat for you." Her eyes twinkled. "Not only are you invited to have dinner with me tonight, but you also get one more joke for today!"

Maya rolled her eyes. "Oh no!"

Grace laughed. "Really. It's not necessary," she protested.

"It is absolutely no problem. I know how much you both like these," Kat insisted. "Here goes: what kind of dog loves to take bubble baths?"

"No. No," Maya said, groaning. "I refuse to listen." She slapped her hands over her ears.

Grace giggled.

Kat tried to look offended. It was difficult when her mouth kept wanting to smile.

"Okay, okay, put us out of our misery," said Maya. "What kind of dog loves to take bubble baths?"

"Why, a shampoodle, of course!" announced Kat.

"So, so bad!" moaned Maya.

"So, so, so bad!" groaned Grace.

ABOUT THE AUTHOR

Award-winning author Susan Hughes has written over thirty books—both fiction and nonfiction—for children of all ages, including *Earth to Audrey, Island Horse, Four Seasons of Patrick, Off to Class: Incredible and Unusual Schools around the World,* and *Case Closed? Nine Mysteries Unlocked by Modern Science.* She is also a freelance editor and writing coach. Susan lives with her family in Toronto, Canada, in a house with a big red door—and wishes it could always be summer. You can visit her at susanhughes.ca.